Jess the Lonely Puppy

Jess the Lonely Puppy

Holly Webb

Illustrated by Sophy Williams

SCHOLASTIC INC.

New York   Toronto   London   Auckland
Sydney   Mexico City   New Delhi   Hong Kong

For Robin and William

ISBN 978-0-545-32574-5

12 11 10 9 8 7 6 5 4 3 2 1   11 12 13 14 15 16/0

Printed in the U.S.A.   40
First Scholastic printing, April 2011

Chapter One

Chloe laughed delightedly as the ducklings squabbled over the bread. It was probably a special treat for them, she decided, as it wasn't just any old bread, but the crusts of her cheese-and-ketchup sandwich. Ducks probably didn't get ketchup very often. She crouched down by the edge of the lake to watch them. The ducklings polished off the last few crumbs, and then circled nearby, in case she had any more. They were so sweet—mostly brown, with yellow streaks and patches, and really fluffy. Their mother was paddling watchfully around them, eyeing Chloe carefully.

A couple of the little ducks were getting braver now, swimming closer and closer. Chloe held her breath as the pair of them clambered onto the muddy edge of the lake with awkward little hops. They were coming to see her! She just wished she had some more sandwich for them. The bravest of the ducklings pecked thoughtfully at the toe of her shoe, but didn't seem very impressed.

"Sorry," she whispered, trying not to

laugh out loud and scare them away. "I don't have anything else!"

Suddenly, there was a scuffling noise and an earsplitting bark. A little black-and-white dog burst through a clump of reeds and nearly knocked Chloe into the lake.

The ducklings squeaked in alarm and leaped back into the water, swimming away as fast as they could, their little feet paddling furiously.

"Oops!" The boy chasing the dog grinned. "Sorry, Chlo, did Jess knock you over?"

"No, I'm just sitting in the mud because I feel like it!" she snapped. She looked out across the lake, watching the mother duck and her babies speeding off into the deeper water, away from the badly behaved dog. She wished she could swim away, too.

Jess watched the ducklings and barked after them happily. She'd never seen ducklings before, and they were very exciting.

"Why isn't she on her leash?" Chloe asked her brother angrily as she struggled to her feet and tried to brush the sticky mud off her denim shorts. "She's not old enough to walk on her own, Mom and Dad said. She might run off and get lost, or get into a fight with another dog."

Will shrugged. "There's no one else here, Chloe; why shouldn't she run around? She's not bothering anyone."

"She's bothering me," Chloe growled. She knew she sounded grumpy and miserable, but she had really been enjoying playing with the ducks, and she'd hoped the bravest one might even have let her pet him.

Will sighed and rolled his eyes, and Jess, bored now that the ducks had disappeared, scrabbled her muddy paws up against Chloe's legs, hoping for some of the bread she could smell.

"Ow! Get her off of me!" Chloe squeaked, dodging sideways and almost falling into the lake. Will grabbed her arm to pull her back, and Chloe shoved him away. Jess jumped around them with earsplitting barks, thinking that this was all a game.

"What's going on? Are you two all right? Chloe, come away from the edge, sweetheart, you might fall in. And I'm not diving after you!"

Chloe and Will's granddad gently pulled them away from the water. Chloe had started crying, and Will looked upset. Jess whined. She wasn't sure what was going on, but suddenly she didn't like this game anymore. She slunk away from the children, and trotted off around the side of the lake.

"Go and get her, Will," Granddad said. "Put her back on her leash. She isn't really old enough to be off the leash yet."

Will chased after Jess, who darted away, glad that this was a game again. Granddad put his arm round Chloe. "What's up? Jess didn't hurt you, did she?"

Chloe shook her head. "She just knocked me over and got me all muddy. But I was watching those ducks, and she chased them all away. Why does she have to be so rough?"

"She's only little, Chloe. Puppies are silly like that. And Jess doesn't know her own strength."

Chloe sniffed and looked over at Jess and Will, who were running back toward them now.

"Why don't you take her for a walk around the lake with Will, once he's got her back on the leash?" Granddad suggested gently. "I'll come, too, if you want."

Chloe hesitated. She wanted to go, if Jess was on the leash. . . . But then the puppy spotted two Canada geese flying overhead and barked at full volume, jumping up and trying to catch the birds, who ignored her completely.

Chloe shrank back against Granddad. "No, it's okay. I'll go back and sit with Mom and Dad and read my book."

Granddad sighed as he watched her run back to her parents, who were sitting on the picnic blanket. He followed after her slowly.

Jess scampered off, and Will laughed as she pulled hard on her leash. She loved walks like this, with lots of different things to sniff out and chase. She caught sight of another duck in the distance and woofed happily, turning back to glance bright-eyed at Will. They raced away excitedly together.

Chloe sat down on the blanket and stared at her book, but she wasn't really reading it. It was a book about a girl and her dog, which was actually pretty funny, she realized. Girls who read dog books were supposed to like dogs, not be scared of them.

Chloe propped her chin on her hands and reread the first line of the page, but she just couldn't concentrate. Why hadn't she gone with Granddad and Will to walk Jess? She had been so excited when Mom and Dad had finally given in and said yes, they could get a puppy. Will and Chloe had been begging them for a long time. It was going to be a family dog who belonged to everyone, even though it was Will who wanted one the most. He was ten now, and Mom and Dad had said that if he was really careful, he and Chloe would be able to take the puppy out on their own, once they'd been to some dog-training classes.

Unluckily, although the Greys had had Jess for six weeks now and she was big enough to go out for full walks, the dog-training classes had clashed with Will's soccer practice. Will didn't mind too much. He and Dad took her for really long walks when Dad got home from work, or sometimes he went with Granddad.

But Chloe didn't go at all. She had been sure that everything would be okay. She couldn't possibly be scared of a tiny little puppy, could she? When they'd had a family discussion to decide what sort of dog they should get, she had said she didn't mind as long as it was friendly and sweet, and not too big. And not a boxer.

A boxer had scared her three years ago, back in first grade. She'd been running after Mom and Will through the park on the way home, and she'd gone too close to the big dog. It had thought she was going to snatch the stick it was playing with and snapped at her. The boxer hadn't really hurt Chloe, just torn her sweater sleeve, but she had been terrified, and Mom had been furious with the dog's owner. She'd told the man that his dog should be on a leash if it wasn't properly trained. She'd said she'd report him to the police if she ever saw it loose in the park again.

Then Mom had explained to Will and Chloe that they shouldn't ever, ever go near strange dogs, even if they looked friendly. Chloe had already known that, of course, but she hadn't meant to upset the dog. She'd just run a little bit too close.

For several months after that, she would beg Mom to take them home from school the long way so they didn't have to go through the park, where there were always people walking dogs. But that had been three years ago. She could walk through the park now, although she wouldn't pet even the friendliest dogs.

Chloe had been certain that a puppy

would be all right. She loved the *idea* of having a dog, and a puppy that she knew from when it was tiny—surely she wouldn't be scared?

But it hadn't worked out like that at all. The first time Chloe had seen Jess, the Border collie puppy was gorgeous —so fluffy, like a little black-and-white ball. They had gone to see the litter of puppies at the breeder's, and Chloe and Will had laughed at the funny little pups climbing over each other and bouncing around their pen. Chloe had been so excited, and when she finally built up the courage to pet the little black-and-white head, Jess had licked her hand with a tiny pink tongue. Chloe had loved her from the start.

She could see Will and Jess now,

playing by the tall trees at the edge of the lake, Jess jumping excitedly at the stick that Will was waving. It was the kind of energetic game Jess loved.

That was Chloe's problem. Jess wasn't just fluffy and sweet. She was jumpy, too, and wriggly and loud. Will played with her all the time, and that made her even more excited. She would jump around his feet, barking away, and Chloe couldn't help looking at her sharp little white teeth. She'd been looking forward to the puppy curling up on her lap for a cuddle sometimes, but Jess just didn't seem to be that sort of dog.

Chloe tried to hide it, but even though she wanted to, she was too scared to touch her. And Jess had Will, who loved her so much. Why would she bother with a girl who never pet her, and pulled away even if Jess just gave her an interested sniff?

Chapter Two

Chloe was half reading and half listening to Granddad and her parents chatting when a loud bark made her jump. She watched as the puppy suddenly appeared from among the trees, streaking toward them in a black-and-white blur.

"She's running around off her leash again," she said nervously.

Mom looked over at Jess. "She's just

having fun, Chloe, don't worry."

Jess stopped a little way away from the picnic blanket and barked again anxiously. She needed them to come now, but they were just staring at her. She pawed at Chloe's leg, but Chloe pulled away with a frightened squeak.

Jess shook her ears impatiently. Why did Chloe always do that? Frantically, she ran back toward the trees a little way and barked again.

"I think something's wrong," Dad said, frowning and getting up. "Where's Will?"

Will! Yes, they'd understood at last! Jess whined again, and then wagged her tail as Dad and Chloe finally followed her. Will had told her to fetch them, and even though she hadn't wanted to leave him, she was desperate to help.

"Oh, no . . . ," Dad muttered as they got closer to the trees. Huddled at the bottom of one of the taller trees was Will. Dad and Chloe broke into a run.

"It's all right, we're here now," Dad said as he crouched down by Will.

"I fell—I got really high up and a branch broke . . . ," Will said faintly.

"Don't worry, you'll be all right," Dad said soothingly. He turned to Chloe. "Go and get your mom and tell her to call an ambulance. I think Will might have broken his leg."

Jess sat in the kitchen in her basket, whimpering every so often. She didn't know what was happening, but things were definitely not right. And she didn't know where Will was.

"Shh, shh, Jess," Granddad said gently, petting her head. "Don't worry. Poor Jess, it must have been very frightening for her, seeing Will like that."

"It was frightening for everybody," Chloe whispered, cupping her hands around her hot chocolate. Granddad had made it for her. He said even though it was summer, there was nothing like hot chocolate when people were upset. But it didn't seem to be working.

"I wish Mom would call." Chloe stared hopefully at the phone, as though that would make it burst into life. "She promised to call as soon as she knew what was happening."

Granddad patted Chloe's hand, just like he'd pet Jess. "I know it was scary, but Will's going to be well looked after. A broken leg heals quickly, and Will's healthy and strong. He was awake and talking to us, that's the important thing."

Chloe nodded. She supposed her granddad was right, but Will's leg had been all twisted and wrong looking.

At last the phone rang, and Chloe spilled her drink all over the table.

Granddad reached for the phone before Chloe could grab it. "Hello, love. What's happening?"

Chloe hovered next to Granddad, trying to hear, but it was mostly just *Mm–hm* and *Right,* from his end. She could hardly hear Mom at all.

Finally, Granddad put down the phone.

"Didn't she want to talk to me?" Chloe asked, sounding hurt.

"She didn't have long, Chlo. Will's going to have an operation on his leg. She needed to be with him."

Chloe gaped at him. "An operation? But I thought he'd just have a cast put on it? Isn't that what you do for broken legs? That's what Maddy had when she broke her arm."

Granddad nodded. "It's a bad break—he fell a long way. He's going to have some special pins put in it, to hold the bone together while it heals. Don't worry, they do it all the time."

"Is Will going to have to stay in the hospital for long?" Chloe asked, tracing patterns in hot chocolate on the plastic tablecloth. She'd wiped it up, but not very well.

Jess came and stood with her paws on Granddad's knee. She could hear them talking about Will. Where was he? When was he coming home?

"For a while," Granddad replied. "Mom wasn't sure. I'm going to stay here for a couple of nights to look after you."

Chloe felt her throat tighten. She had thought Will would be home tonight. Staying in the hospital sounded scary.

Jess looked at Chloe. Was she worried about Will? What was going on? She whimpered, staring up at Chloe and Granddad hopefully. But Chloe just turned away and walked quickly out of the room, her eyes filling with tears.

"Let her calm down," Granddad murmured to Jess.

Jess stared up at him with big, sad eyes. Everyone was upset, and the house felt strange without Will. She wanted him to come home and play fetch with her in the yard.

Granddad sighed and tickled her

behind the ears. "I know, Jess. I want him home, too. But it's just going to be us for a while."

The last week of the school year was usually a lot of fun. But this year, everything seemed different. Will and Chloe normally walked to school together, because it was just around the corner, and Will was in fifth grade and old enough to be responsible, Mom said. But all that week, Chloe had to walk to school with Granddad, because she couldn't go by herself. Jess came, too, because Granddad said she really needed some exercise.

Chloe missed Will, and Mom and Dad, too. They were spending a lot of time at the hospital with Will, and Granddad was going to stay at Chloe's house for the rest of the week to help. She loved Granddad, but she couldn't help feeling left out. At least she had pony camp to look forward to. She and her friend Maddy were spending the second week of the summer staying at a riding center, where they'd each get to look after their own special pony all week. They'd be going riding and they'd be learning to jump, too. Chloe couldn't wait.

Maddy met them halfway to school, as usual. She knew all about Chloe's problems with Jess, but she adored dogs.

"She's so wonderful," Maddy told

Chloe as Jess trotted alongside them. "I do know what you mean about her being a little wild, but she's so cute!"

Chloe sighed. Even though Maddy was her best friend, and she was trying really hard to understand how Chloe felt about Jess, she just couldn't. Maddy loved dogs almost as much as Will!

On Tuesday after school, Mom picked Chloe up in the car to take her to visit Will. She'd seen him for five minutes the day before, but he'd still been sleepy after the operation, and she wasn't sure he'd really known she was there. Chloe was desperate to see him, but nervous at the same time. She knew he was bound to ask about Jess, and she didn't know what to say.

Chloe was starting to worry about the puppy. She spent most of her time moping in her basket, or perched on the window seat in the living room, where she usually sat to watch for Will walking home from school. Obviously, she was waiting for him to come, and whenever she heard Mom or Dad pulling up in the car she would rush to the door, barking excitedly, her plumy tail wagging. Then as soon as she realized Will wasn't with them, she would slink sadly back to her basket.

Will had a big cast on his leg, but otherwise he was his old self. Except that he hated having to keep still.

Chloe perched on the edge of Will's bed while Mom went over to speak to one of the nurses.

"I can't believe it. I'm going to be stuck in bed forever!" he groaned.

"Does it hurt?" Chloe asked, biting her lip.

"No, it's all right, I've got medicine to stop it from hurting. It's itchy, though." Will frowned. "Chloe, how's Jess? Does she miss me? Mom says she's fine, but I think she's just saying anything to make me feel better."

Chloe glanced over at Mom, who was still talking to the nurse. She knew what he meant. But she didn't want to upset Will, either. Worrying about Jess would only make him feel worse.

"She's okay," Chloe said carefully. "She does miss you, but Granddad's taking her for walks, and she comes with us to school and back."

"But Granddad can't run, Chloe. He's too old! Jess needs a lot of exercise. And I was supposed to take her to dog training this summer." He looked worried. "Couldn't you go for walks with Granddad?" Will pleaded. "I know you're nervous with Jess, but if Granddad was there, too . . ."

Chloe looked at her fingers. "We all walk to school together," she repeated. But she knew that wasn't really what Will meant.

"Come on, Chloe. Will needs to rest now. You can come back and see him soon." Mom had finished talking, and was looking at Will's pale face with concern.

Chloe hardly spoke on the way home, until they were just turning onto their street. "How long is Will going to be there for?" she asked suddenly.

"I'm really not sure, Chloe," Mom answered. "He should have been able to come home after the operation, but the nurse said they're worried that the bone pieces haven't fit back together yet. It could be a while—a few weeks, even."

"Weeks?" Chloe whispered in horror. She hadn't thought it could possibly be that long. She would miss his bad jokes. And Jess would be heartbroken.

The puppy was waiting hopefully by the door when they got in, and her drooping ears made Chloe feel so guilty. She'd said to Will that Jess was okay, but now she looked so miserable. Chloe sighed. If she'd told Will that, it would have made him miserable, too. There was nothing he could do about it, stuck in the hospital.

But I could help, Chloe told herself. *I could try and cheer Jess up.*

She followed Jess into the kitchen, and watched as she slumped down into her basket. Chloe felt so sorry for her, sitting there with her head hanging.

"Hey, Jess," she said gently, crouching down by the basket.

Jess ignored her. She wanted Will, and he still hadn't come back to her. She didn't like it when he went to school every day, but at least he always came home. Where was he now? And why hadn't he taken her with him?

Chloe nervously darted out a hand

to pat Jess, but she patted her too hard, when Jess wasn't expecting it.

Jess was feeling so upset that when Chloe touched her, she jumped around and barked sharply, showing her teeth. What was going on? She stared angrily at Chloe, who was scrambling away, crying. Silly girl!

Why couldn't Chloe just leave her alone?

Chapter Three

Chloe kept away from Jess after that. Her behavior had brought back all those bad memories of the dog in the park. Chloe visited Will, and spoke to him on the phone a couple of times, but whenever he asked her about Jess, she just said that Granddad was taking her for a lot of walks and wriggled out of saying any more.

Granddad really loved dogs, and Jess liked him, but it wasn't the same as racing all over the park with Will. The puppy was bursting with energy, and a couple of short walks a day just weren't enough. Jess was used to a quick walk before school, and then another really long one with Will and Dad later on. But Dad was working late so he could fit in visiting Will at the hospital. He didn't have much time for dog walking. Collies needed so much exercise and Jess really hated being stuck in the house. She was bored.

It was the first morning of the summer, so Jess hadn't even had her walk to school. She wandered around the house with her leash, looking hopeful, but Mom was busy sorting out some books to take to Will, and Jess knew Chloe wouldn't take her. Mom had encouraged Jess to go out into the yard, but that was no fun without someone to play with. She looked around the kitchen, trying to find something interesting to do. She pushed her squeaky bone across the floor for a while, but what she really needed was Will to throw it for her to chase.

Her bone was up against the kitchen cupboards now, so Jess scrabbled with one paw to get it back into the middle of the floor. But her claws caught on the cupboard door instead. It opened a little way, and then bounced shut.

Jess stared at it, fascinated. Then she carefully hooked her claws around the edge of the door once more. Again, the door bounced and banged.

The next time, she pulled it a little too hard, and it didn't bang back. Jess went to nudge the door again with her nose, but then she caught a delicious and interesting whiff from the cupboard.

There was food in there. Jess used her nose to push the door open farther and found the cereal boxes.

"Oh, no! Mo-om!" Chloe was standing in the kitchen doorway, staring at Jess, who looked back guiltily. She was surrounded by chewed-up cardboard and an awful lot of cornflakes.

"What's the matter? Oh, Jess!" Mom had come downstairs and was gazing at the mess in horror. "You bad dog," she said, annoyed. "What a waste. I hope you're not going to get sick now."

Jess flattened herself to the floor and whined miserably, backing toward her basket. She hadn't meant to be bad. The cereal had smelled so good, and the cardboard boxes had been fun to tear up with her teeth. . . .

Mom sighed. "Oh, Jess. It isn't really your fault. You need a walk, don't you?"

Jess thumped her tail on the floor, just once, but she kept down, watching Mom clean up the mess. She *was* sorry, but she still felt grumpy and bored. She desperately wanted something to do.

Chloe helped her mom to clean up. When they'd finished, Mom gave her a hug. "Not the best way to spend the first day of the summer, is it? Would you like to go out for ice cream together after we go to see Will this afternoon? I feel like I've hardly seen you recently."

Chloe hugged her back, nearly spilling a dustpan full of cornflakes. "Yes, please! Thanks, Mom!" She danced over to empty the cornflakes in the garbage. "Don't worry about having to go to the hospital so much. I'll be at pony camp next week with Maddy, so you won't need to worry about me then."

She turned around smiling, but her eyes widened as she saw her mother's face. "What is it?"

"Oh, Chloe! I never called them! I was supposed to do it the day after Will had his accident, and I never called them to register!" Mom looked horrified. "Where's the brochure? I'll call them now."

She grabbed the phone, and Chloe watched her make the call. Her mom frowned a little as she explained, and then looked terribly disappointed and guilty. Chloe knew what Mom was going to say before she even put down the phone.

"I'm so sorry. They're all booked up. They've promised to call me if there's a cancellation, but they didn't sound very hopeful. Oh, Chlo, I feel terrible. . . ."

Chloe stared down at the ground. She wanted to say it was okay; she knew Mom had had other things on her mind. But she had been looking forward to this for so long! She and Maddy had talked about it every day at school, drawing pictures of the ponies they might get to take care of. How was she going to tell Maddy? It would ruin her vacation, too!

She swallowed hard, trying not to yell at Mom. She knew she hadn't done it on purpose. But it was so unfair!

She dashed out of the kitchen, scrambled up the stairs to her room, and flung herself onto her bed, crying.

Mom spent all this time worrying about Will, and she'd just forgotten about her. She mattered, too, didn't she?

She cried so much that her head ached, and then she actually fell asleep, in the middle of the day.

Mom came in just after she'd woken up, which made Chloe think she'd probably been hanging around outside her room for a while. She had a plate with a sandwich and some chips on it.

"You missed lunch," she said gently. "Cheese and ketchup, look." It was Chloe's favorite. She wiped her eyes and took the plate gratefully.

"I spoke to Maddy's mom and explained. I said I'd arrange something really special for you girls later in the summer."

Chloe just nodded.

"I really am sorry, Chlo."

She looked sorry, and Chloe leaned against her shoulder. Crying made her feel awful, and she felt guilty now as well. At least she wasn't stuck in the hospital like Will. "I know," she muttered.

"Are you still going to come with me to visit Will tonight?" Mom asked. "I know he's looking forward to seeing you. He asked if you could bring him some DS games."

Chloe nodded. "Mmm. I know which ones he likes. I'll find them after I eat."

"Thanks, Chlo. You're a star." Mom kissed the top of her head and went back downstairs.

Chloe didn't feel like a star. She felt lonely and miserable. She ate the chips, but she didn't really enjoy them, and then she got up to go and fetch Will's games from his bedroom.

She was searching through the pile on his shelf when a tiny noise made her turn around sharply.

She hadn't noticed that Jess was lying

on Will's bed, staring at her, her eyes looking even darker than usual and so sad. For once, Chloe didn't feel that horrible jump of fright that she got when a dog was too close. Jess just seemed so unhappy.

"You look like I feel . . . ," Chloe joked, but it wasn't really funny. "Mom isn't angry at you anymore, Jess, honestly."

Jess gazed at Chloe, and thought she looked sad, too. She whined, and Chloe nodded.

"I know. You miss Will, don't you?" Chloe picked up the games, then wriggled herself over to lean against Will's bed. "Me, too, Jess."

Jess gave a huge sigh, and Chloe giggled. "That was right in my ear." She looked at Jess, whose nose was hanging over the edge of the bed right next to her, and very gently pet her.

Jess closed her eyes and sighed again, gratefully, as Chloe scratched behind her ears. It felt so nice to have somebody make a fuss over her.

Chloe lay in bed that night feeling too hot to sleep. Mom had said she thought it might thunder, but even though a storm would probably cool everything down, Chloe hoped she was wrong. She hated thunderstorms. She turned over and yawned. She was tired, but she was never going to be able to sleep in this sticky room. . . .

She was woken hours later by a huge

crash of thunder. Her room was still lit up by lightning, which meant the storm was right overhead. Chloe sat up, clutching the blanket around her shoulders. Another flash! The horrible blue-white light sent everything into scary shadows, and she shivered, waiting for the thunder.

Suddenly, a little black-and-white body hurtled through her bedroom door, making Chloe squeak with surprise. Jess flung herself onto Chloe's bed, whimpering in fear.

"Oh, Jess, are you scared of thunder, too?" Chloe cuddled the puppy close, forgetting to be frightened, either of Jess or the thunder. As the next thunderclap cracked overhead, Jess cowered against her, letting Chloe wrap her arms around her small black ears to shut out the noise. "Shhhh, shhhh, it's okay. It'll go away soon."

Jess licked her hand gratefully. She couldn't have stayed in the kitchen, not with those crashing noises and that awful prickly feeling in the air. She really wanted Will, but Chloe would do. It was nice to be cuddled, and she was making good sounds, shushing noises that made the crashing seem not so bad.

She could feel Chloe's heart thudding so quickly. She was scared, too, Jess thought. She licked her again, and then snuggled closer as another growl of thunder rumbled around the house.

Chloe lay there, jumping every so often as the thunder rang out, but mostly thinking over and over, *I'm cuddling Jess. I'm holding a dog! I'd never have thought that she'd be scared of thunder, when she's so bouncy and loud.* "You're even worse than me, Jess." She giggled, and Jess licked her under the chin.

The thunder was dying away now to just a few grumbles, and Chloe lay back down with Jess still cuddled up next to her. "Are you staying, Jess?" she asked.

But Jess was asleep already, curled in a little ball in the crook of Chloe's arm.

Chapter Four

Jess was still there when Chloe woke up the next morning, snuggling with her in bed. Chloe smiled delightedly—it was just like she'd imagined having a dog would be. Jess yawned, showing a huge length of pink tongue, and rolled over onto her back, still fast asleep. She lay there with her paws folded on her chest, snoring a little, until Chloe woke her up by giggling too much.

"Sorry, Jess. You looked so funny."

Jess let out another enormous yawn, then gave Chloe a big face-washing lick.

"Urgh. Now I'm really awake." Chloe got out of bed and followed Jess downstairs to the kitchen, where Mom was making toast.

"I was wondering where Jess was!" Mom said, looking slightly surprised. "You slept late! I was just about to come and wake you up. It's time to go to the library."

Chloe nodded. Her mom worked part-time at the library, and so in the mornings during the summer she and Will usually went with her. Even though she didn't normally hang around with

Will—he stuck with the boys, mostly—it would feel weird being there without him.

Jess watched sadly through the front window as they got into the car without her. She'd been hoping for a walk. She had that itchy, bored feeling again. She trotted back into the kitchen and out into the yard through her dog door. She sniffed around for a while and snapped at a few butterflies, then she just lay on her side in a sunny patch, flicking her tail idly.

A beetle wandered past her nose, and Jess turned over to stare at it as it rolled off between her paws. She crept after it, tail wagging slightly, and watched it climb under some stones in the flower bed. Where had it gone?

Jess pawed at the stones, but the beetle was gone. She scrabbled some more, then dug furiously, her paws spraying up stones and dirt. The beetle was long gone, but the digging was fun. Jess happily clawed and scraped and scratched, loving the exercise.

Then she fell asleep, her nose in a pile of dirt, worn out and snoozing blissfully.

"Jess!"

Jess sat up with a jump, blinking sleepily, and saw that Chloe was there, looking down at her with her hands over her mouth.

"Oh, Jess, Mom's going to go crazy. Dad gave her that plant for her birthday." Chloe quickly fetched a shovel from the yard shed to scoop some of the soil back into the flower bed. "We have to clean up. Maybe she won't notice."

But it was too late. Chloe's mom was standing by the back door, looking horrified. In fact, she looked more than horrified, she looked furious.

"You bad dog! Look at this mess! Oh, I don't believe it! My beautiful camellia . . ." She crouched down to look at the plants that Jess had rooted up.

Jess hung her head sadly. She'd only been playing. . . .

"I think she was bored, Mom," Chloe said quickly. "Don't be mad at her, please. She misses Will, and all the walks he and Dad used to take her on. And now Granddad's not staying here anymore, so she's hardly getting any exercise at all."

Chloe pet Jess, feeling her shiver. It was obvious she hated being shouted at. Chloe frowned. "Mom, could me and Maddy take Jess for a walk? Just to the park. We could run around with her and work off some of her energy; I'm sure she wouldn't be so naughty then."

Mom shook her head. "You're not old enough, Chlo. And I thought you were terrified of dogs! And Jess is such a handful. But you're right, she does need more exercise."

Chloe helped her try to fill in the dirt around the camellia again. "Mom, you let Will walk me to school all last year, and he's only a year older than me. And I'll be with Maddy, too! She'll help me with Jess. We'll be fine!"

Her mom sighed. "Well, it might be worth a try. I'm sure she's only being naughty because we're not spending enough time with her."

Chloe threw her arms around Mom. "Excellent! I'll go and call Maddy!"

"This is great, Chloe. I can't believe you aren't scared of Jess anymore." Maddy was looking admiringly at Chloe walking with Jess on her leash.

Chloe smiled. "I can't, either. But I'm glad it's true."

Jess was scampering along happily, sniffing the interesting smells and hoping they were going to the park so she could run really fast, like she did with Will. She still wished he would come back, but Chloe was her person now, too. Chloe had looked after her during that horrible, frightening night, and that made her special.

They raced all over the park for a whole hour, until the girls were exhausted, although Jess was still bright and bouncy.

"She's not tired at all!" Maddy panted, collapsing onto a bench. "Look at her, she wants to dash off again!"

Jess barked excitedly. She could see a

squirrel scurrying along between those trees, and she loved chasing squirrels. She looked up hopefully at Chloe and tugged on the leash.

"Sorry, Jess, we've got to get home. I promised Mom we'd be back by five." Chloe turned to walk Jess out of the park, and Jess gave the squirrel a last longing look before following her.

But then the squirrel changed direction and started to run along the grass almost in front of Jess's nose. It was too much to bear. She gave an enormous bark and flung herself after the squirrel.

Chloe gasped as she felt the leash almost pulling out of her hand. "Hey! Jess, no. Come back!"

Jess was so strong. Chloe tried

desperately to get her under control, but she was only just managing to hold on as Jess dragged her after the squirrel. They galloped over the grass, and then Jess cut across one of the paved paths that ran through the park. Chloe tripped on the edge of the grass and went flying, finally letting go of her leash.

Jess sped up. She was going to catch a squirrel at last! But the squirrel had made it to the trees, and all Jess could do was bark at it as it disappeared into the leafy branches. Disappointed, she turned to go back to Chloe.

Chloe! There she was, lying on the path. She was crying! Jess let out a terrified whimper and raced over, throwing herself onto the ground next to Chloe and whining miserably.

Chloe had scraped her knee on the cement, and blood was dripping down her leg. Maddy was trying to wipe it up with a tissue, but it was a nasty cut.

"Oh, Jess, it's okay." Chloe sniffed. "Don't be upset." She could see why Jess was frightened, and she felt so sorry for her. Will had been hurt, and he'd gone away. Now Jess thought that she was going to go away, too.

"Are you all right to walk?" Maddy asked, helping Chloe to her feet.

"I'm fine," Chloe said. "Let's go home."

Maddy took Jess by the leash. "Just don't go too fast, Jess, okay?"

They slowly made their way back, with Chloe leaning on Maddy and Jess trotting obediently alongside her.

Chloe's mom was watching out for them through the front window. She looked worried.

"Are we really late?" Chloe muttered.

Maddy frowned. "A bit. And she wasn't sure about letting us go, was she?"

Mom flung open the front door. "Chloe, you promised me five—Oh, no, what have you done?" She helped Chloe inside, and Jess and Maddy crept in behind them, not wanting to be noticed.

"What happened?" Mom asked, getting down the first-aid kit. She looked very upset—much more upset than she ought to be about just a scraped knee, Chloe thought.

"Jess ran after a squirrel and I tripped," she explained, trying not to make it sound too serious.

"That dog again!" Mom said angrily.

"She didn't mean to hurt me! She was really sorry—she was whimpering," Chloe protested. But she could see Mom wasn't really listening.

"She's too wild. I don't know what we're going to do with her," Mom said,

dabbing at Chloe's knee with a wipe.

"Oh, she isn't really, Mom!" Chloe protested, giving Maddy a horrified look. "She's lovely! She didn't mean to hurt me."

Jess sat in her basket, her eyes swiveling between Mom and Chloe, shivering at the loud, upset voices. Mom kept looking at her as though this was all her fault. And Jess had a horrible feeling that it was.

Chapter Five

Will smiled and shook his head as he spotted Chloe walking up the children's ward, a big bandage on her knee. "I know you miss me, Chlo, but cutting your leg off so you can stay in the hospital, too, that's just crazy. . . . Seriously, what did you do?"

Chloe grinned at him. "I took Jess for a walk! Well, me and Maddy did."

She looked down at the bandage and shrugged. "But Jess wanted to chase a squirrel, and I tripped. . . ."

Will beamed. "That's fantastic!"

"Hey!"

"Not your knee! Fantastic that you took Jess out. Thanks, Chlo. I'd been really worried about her."

Chloe sighed and glanced over at her mom, who was talking to the doctor. "I'm not sure Mom's going to let me take her out again, though," she whispered. "She was so mad. Jess has been really naughty the last couple of days."

Will thought for a moment. "Well, if you really can't talk Mom into it, maybe you can wear off some of Jess's energy in the yard. She loves playing fetch, and you could try hiding one of her toys and getting her to play hide-and-seek—that's fun. Then maybe she'll be less energetic."

Chloe nodded. "Good idea. Anyway, I might still get Mom to give in."

"You just need to stretch your legs, don't you, Jess?" Chloe murmured, stroking Jess's silky black-and-white back, as they leaned against the sofa watching TV.

Jess let out a huge sigh, as if in agreement, then slumped down with her head in Chloe's lap.

Chloe had worked hard at persuading her mom that Jess had only tripped her up by accident. But Mom was still saying that she didn't think it was a good idea for Chloe and Maddy to take Jess out again. Chloe was also worried about what her mom had said about not knowing what to do with Jess. What did that mean? She was scared that her mom might want to send Jess back to the breeder they'd gotten her from. Will would be heartbroken.

And it wasn't just Will. Chloe would miss Jess so much, too, she realized now. She was determined to turn Jess into the most perfect dog ever, so Mom wouldn't want to get rid of her. But that meant they had to go out for more walks. Chloe was sure that Jess was only acting out because she needed lots more exercise, and the occasional short walks she was getting with Granddad just weren't enough. She'd spent the morning playing in the yard with Jess, like Will had suggested, but she was sure that Jess really wanted more space for a good long run.

Eventually, after a whole day of begging, Mom agreed to let Chloe and Maddy take Jess out. But she made Chloe take her cell phone, so they could call home if anything went wrong.

Luckily, Jess seemed to know that she had to be on her best behavior. She walked sedately all the way to the park, trotting along next to Chloe. Chloe and Maddy smiled at each other as a couple of old ladies commented on what a well-behaved dog she was.

"I wish we could get them to go and

say that to my mom!" Chloe whispered,
and Maddy giggled.

Chloe's leg was still a bit too sore for
her to run really fast, so Maddy took
Jess's leash when they got to the park.

Jess looked up at Maddy and Chloe, her ears pricked, but she didn't race off.

"What's up, Jess?" Maddy asked her gently.

Chloe leaned down to pet her, and Jess nuzzled her gently, pressing her cool, damp nose into Chloe's hand. She rubbed Jess's ears. "It's okay, Jess. You go! Run with Maddy!"

"But not too fast!" Maddy added, smiling.

Jess wagged her tail delightedly, swishing it like a flag, and sprinted away, but she kept coming back to check on Chloe, who was sitting on one of the benches.

"She's really worried about you," Maddy said, panting. Jess had just raced to the other side of the trees and back.

"She's such a sweetheart."

Jess sat on the path, laid her muzzle on Chloe's lap, and stared up at her anxiously. Was Chloe all right? She swept her tail back and forth across the path when Chloe beamed at her.

Maddy flopped onto the bench, too. "We should head back, shouldn't we?" she asked, checking her watch.

Chloe nodded. "Let's go home past the shops to give Jess a change," she suggested. She took the leash from Maddy and got to her feet.

Jess looked up at them both, and her tail stopped wagging. Home? Already? But she wanted to run some more! That had hardly felt like a walk at all.

"Do you think your mom will let you take Jess out on your own next week, when I'm at pony camp?" Maddy asked, as they walked through the park gates.

Chloe frowned. She hadn't really thought about that. "I haven't mentioned it yet, but I can't see her saying yes. She'd be too worried something might happen to us. Maybe I can ask Granddad to come with me. . . ."

"Do you mind if I run in and buy a magazine?" Maddy asked, as they went past the corner shop.

Chloe shook her head. "Of course not. We'll wait for you outside. Sit, Jess!"

Jess looked at Chloe doubtfully, and Chloe gently pushed her to sit down. She'd been reading up on the Internet about dog training, and she'd tried practicing with Jess in the yard, but they weren't very good at it yet. Eventually, Jess sat, and Chloe fussed over her lovingly.

Maddy took a while. Chloe could see her through the window, trying to decide which magazine to buy.

She gazed down at her feet, thinking sadly about pony camp and how cool it would have been. But then, if she'd gone, Jess would have been really lonely without her, she supposed. Maybe it was all for the best.

Jess got bored of sitting still and watching people going in and out of the shop. Lots of them had interesting things in their bags, though. She sniffed hopefully. Delicious-smelling things.

Suddenly, Jess pulled sharply at her

leash, and Chloe gasped as she dragged it out of her hand. Before Chloe could catch her, Jess was right outside the shop door, rooting through a big shopping bag which a lady had put down while she found her car keys.

"Jess, no!" Chloe squeaked, horrified, as the lady tried to pull her bag away.

"Is this your dog?" she demanded furiously. "What on earth were you doing, letting go of her like that?"

"I'm really sorry!" Chloe said, blushing. "Oh, Jess . . ." She finally managed to grab Jess's leash and pull her out of the shopping bag, but it was too late. She had some meat in her mouth, and there was a package sticking out of the bag, ripped open by her sharp little teeth.

"She's eating my food!" the lady shouted. Chloe thought she might explode, she looked so angry.

"I'm so sorry, I'll pay for it," she gasped, frantically digging in her skirt pocket for her money, while trying to hold on to Jess's collar with her other hand.

Jess had finished the delicious food, but she was beginning to realize that she'd done something wrong. The lady with the bag was shouting at Chloe. Jess squirmed behind Chloe's legs to hide.

Chloe quickly pressed a few dollars into the lady's hand, muttering, "Sorry!" again. As she pulled Jess away, she could hear the lady behind her, telling everyone coming out of the shop that little girls shouldn't be allowed to walk dogs they couldn't control.

"What happened?" said Maddy, as she came out of the shop, clutching her magazine.

"Jess stole that lady's food!" Chloe whispered to her friend. "It was so embarrassing! I don't think I'll ever go in that shop again!"

When they got home, Chloe carefully avoided telling Mom about their walk—except that Jess had been good in the park. She went out into the yard and lay on the picnic blanket under the apple tree in the shade. It was so hot.

Jess lay down next to her, panting and wagging her tail as the bees buzzed past her nose.

Chloe reached out to pet her. "What am I going to do with you, Jess?" she muttered. "Only two walks. One cut knee for me, one stolen meal for you. This isn't working out very well, is it?"

Chapter Six

Granddad came over the next day to look after Chloe while Mom and Dad went to the hospital, and as soon as they'd shut the front door behind them, Chloe pulled him over to the kitchen table to sit down and talk.

"What's the matter, Chlo?" Granddad grinned at her. "You're looking very serious."

Chloe huffed out a sigh. "It is serious! I've tried everything, but Jess can't stop getting into trouble. Mom's really angry at her, and I'm worried she might take her back to the dog breeder."

Granddad looked down at Jess, who was fighting with her stretchy rubber bone under the table. "I'm sure your mom wouldn't do that. She hasn't said anything to me. What's Jess been doing?"

Chloe explained about the cereal, and the plants, and her knee, and then the stolen meat. It did sound awful when it was all in a long list, she realized.

Granddad nodded slowly. "I didn't know she was so upset with Jess, but I can see why. . . . It's been really hard for her and your dad, you know, worrying so much about Will. And they're worried about you, too, Chlo. Your mom thinks it's really spoiling your summer."

"If I could get Jess to behave well and go for walks without being afraid of what she might do, I'd be having a perfect summer," Chloe replied.

"But you're already making a big difference," Granddad pointed out, reaching across the table to cover her hand with his. "Think back to the day of Will's accident—just think about how you were with Jess. I felt so sad, watching you. It looked like you secretly wanted to play with Jess and Will, but you couldn't make yourself. And now look at you! I know the walks didn't turn out too well, but at least you went! And you haven't given up on Jess, even after she's gotten you into trouble. I'm so proud of you."

Chloe went pink and looked down at the table, feeling embarrassed. Dad had spotted her cuddling Jess the day before and told her it was great that she seemed to be getting along so well with the puppy, but no one had said it as nicely as that before.

"But it isn't making her any better behaved, Granddad. I just don't know what to try next."

Granddad hugged her. "Honestly, your mom won't send her back. But we don't want her getting any more stressed out than she is already." He nodded thoughtfully. "What that dog needs is a training class."

"Oh, yes!" Chloe bounced in her chair. "Will was going to take her, but it clashed with soccer. He was planning to do it over the summer instead, but then we all forgot about it after the accident."

"How about it, then? You, me, and Jess. Let's find ourselves a trainer. Come on, Chlo, show me some of those computer skills. Let's go and see what's around here."

Ten minutes later, Chloe and Granddad had found a training class that was being run in the church hall around the corner. "Look, there's a class starting this Tuesday," Granddad pointed out. "Perfect. Something fun for us to do while Maddy's away, to stop you from feeling too sad about that pony club thingamabob."

"Pony camp." Chloe giggled. "Can we call now, Granddad? I hope they aren't full."

Luckily, they weren't. Granddad put down the phone, looking very pleased with himself.

"We can go?" Chloe asked eagerly. She was standing next to him, with Jess waltzing excitedly at her legs. Jess could tell that something good was happening. Chloe sounded so happy.

Granddad nodded. "And when I told Mike, the trainer, that Jess was a Border collie, he mentioned that he does agility sessions, too. So I've signed us up for a preview class in a few weeks' time."

"What's agility?" Chloe asked,

stooping down to hug Jess and ruffling the fur around her neck. Jess looked up at her adoringly.

"Haven't you ever seen it on TV?" Granddad replied. "It's like show jumping, but for dogs. Jess isn't old enough for real agility classes yet, but Mike thought she'd enjoy the preview session."

Chloe beamed. "Jess would love that."

"I'm sure she would. Mike said it's great for collies; it works off lots of their energy. I thought it sounded just like what we need!"

Chloe was nervous about the first training session. What if Jess didn't behave? It would be really embarrassing if she just wouldn't do as she was told. And Chloe was a tiny bit worried about all those other dogs. She wasn't scared of Jess anymore, but she wasn't sure how she'd feel about a room full of dogs.

Luckily, there were only five in their class, and they were all puppies, too. Two Labradors, one black and one chocolate, a cocker spaniel, and one breed that Chloe didn't recognize. His owner said he was a mixed bag.

Jess enjoyed the class. Everyone fussed over her and said how beautiful she was, and Chloe kept telling her she was a good dog every time she did as she was told.

"She's doing really well." Mike, the trainer, crouched down by Jess and patted her gently. "Let's see you walk up the room, turn at the end, and come back. Don't pull her, and walk slowly, okay? Lots of praise."

Chloe looked down at Jess lovingly— "Come on, Jess, walk," she said, keeping her voice gentle but firm, like she'd been told.

Jess showed off happily, trotting along right next to Chloe and turning perfectly, without Chloe having to pull her.

"Great. Give her one of your treats, Chloe. She's a natural." Mike looked really pleased.

"You are such a clever girl, Jess!" Chloe said, holding out a dog biscuit.

Jess gulped down the delicious meaty biscuit, wagging her tail happily. She loved dog training!

At the end of the class, Granddad walked over. He'd been watching from the back of the room, and Chloe had asked him to take some photos to show Will when she went to visit.

"We were so lucky there was a course starting this week. Jess seemed to really enjoy herself." Granddad smiled. "I'm sure she'll love that agility session, too."

On their way home, Jess walked close to Chloe, feeling happily tired after the class. She wanted to go home and curl up in her basket, then later maybe Chloe would play those fun games with her in the yard.

There might even be more of the yummy treats.

Chloe's mom was delighted that it had gone so well. "I'm going to have to come and watch one of these classes," she suggested. "It sounds as though you and Jess are doing wonderfully."

"We've got beginner's training on Tuesdays and Thursdays for the next four weeks," Chloe explained.

"Are you coming with me to see Will?" Mom asked.

Chloe nodded excitedly. "Yes, I want to tell him how fantastic Jess was at the class. He's going to be so proud of her! I didn't tell him we were going, in case Jess behaved really badly."

Will was watching a DVD on the screen above his bed, but he turned it off as soon as he saw Mom and Chloe. "Wow, it's good to see you," he said, grinning. "Mom, did they say how much longer I have to be in for?"

Mom shook her head. "I'm supposed to talk to Dr. Bedford today. Hopefully not much longer, now that you've started physical therapy."

Will made a face. "It's good being allowed to move, but I'm so slow! It's going to be a while before I can go for runs in the park with Jess. How is she?"

Chloe beamed at him and pulled out her camera to show him the photos Granddad had taken. "She's awesome! Look!"

Will stared at them, frowning. "You

took her to dog training? But I was going to do that!"

Chloe looked at him in surprise. She had thought he'd be pleased. "I know, but—"

"I was really looking forward to it!" Will said angrily. "She's my dog!"

"Actually, Will, she's a family dog," Mom said gently. "I know you've spent the most time with her, but Chloe's been looking after her really well. You'll be able to go to the classes, too, when you're better."

But Will was still scowling, and he hardly spoke to Chloe for the rest of the visit.

Chapter Seven

When Jess slipped into Chloe's room that night, she could feel that something wasn't right. Ever since Chloe had come home, she'd been so quiet. She'd petted Jess and played with her, but she hadn't been quite the same.

Jess stood by Chloe's bed and looked up hopefully.

"Hello, Jess!" Chloe smiled and patted the blanket. "Come on! Up!"

Jess bounced onto the bed and settled herself on Chloe's tummy, staring into her face. "Oof, you're heavy," Chloe said. "It's nice, though. You're like the best sort of teddy bear." She sighed.

Jess put her head to one side and whined questioningly. What was wrong?

"I know you don't really understand, but you're a very good listener," Chloe murmured, tickling her under the chin.

Jess wagged her tail sleepily and closed her eyes. She was still listening, but she was worn out after all that hard work at the class.

"I hadn't really thought about it until we went to the hospital this evening,"

Chloe said, gazing at the ceiling. "Of course I'm still looking forward to Will coming home, but it's going to be hard when he comes back, too."

Jess flicked one ear thoughtfully as Chloe mentioned Will.

"I know Mom said you're a family dog, but really you've always been mostly his. You're not going to want to play with me once you've got Will back. . . ."

Chloe sighed and looked down at Jess again. "I'm not even sure we can keep going to dog training. Will was so upset. . . ." Then she smiled sadly. Jess was fast asleep, floppy as a rag doll, stretched out on her tummy.

"I'll make the most of my time with you while I can," she whispered, petting Jess lovingly.

Granddad was very firm with Chloe when she suggested giving up the dog-training classes until Will could take Jess instead.

"No. Absolutely not, Chlo. That's not fair to you or Jess. You saw how much she loved training, and she needs it, too. She was getting into bad habits. It's sad for Will, but he loves Jess, and he'll understand. There'll be plenty more classes that he can take her to. I'm going to see him this afternoon, so I'll have a chat with him."

Chloe hugged him with relief. She really didn't want to give up the classes —that first one had been so much fun.

When she next went to see Will, he

glared at her as she came up to his bed, and she wondered if he was still mad.

"Granddad says I have to say sorry," Will muttered grumpily. "He says I should be grateful to you for looking after Jess so well." He sighed. "And I am. It's only that I was really looking forward to the classes. But Jess needs training now. I know it's not fair to make her wait."

Chloe beamed at him. "You'll be out of here soon, then you can take her. She's really good," she added.

It was true. They'd gone to quite a few classes now, since they were twice a week, and Jess was a star at every one. There was going to be a competition at the final training session, Mike had said, and Chloe really wanted Jess to do well. They'd been practicing lots in the yard. She didn't mention training to Will again, though; it didn't seem very fair.

She just wished Will could have come to the special agility session, too. As she and Granddad watched Mike setting up the course, she knew he would have loved it.

Mike had brought his two adult Border collies to show everybody else what to do. "Aren't they beautiful?" Chloe whispered to Jess. "You're going to look like them when you're bigger."

Jess wasn't really listening. She was staring eagerly at Mike as he took one of the collies, Marlo, to the start of the course. It had been set up in a big field on a nearby farm.

Jess's tail was twitching with excitement and her eyes sparkled as she watched Marlo set off, speeding around the course, leaping over the jumps, darting in and out of the weaving poles, and shooting through a long pop-up tunnel. He even jumped through a hoop, and then finished by running up a seesaw and tipping it down. Everyone clapped when he and Mike completed the course, and Marlo just shook his ears proudly, as if to say it was nothing.

Mike and another instructor then began to demonstrate how to use the different equipment. Chloe and Jess started with low jumps. Even though Jess was tiny compared to some of the other dogs, she flew over the jumps easily.

Mike watched her, laughing. "Chloe, promise me, when Jess is a year old and can go to real agility classes, you'll bring her along."

"Oh, does she have to be a year?" Chloe asked disappointedly.

Mike nodded. "Some of the agility equipment isn't suitable for pups because they're still growing. Things like the weaving poles—those sticks Marlo was going in and out of—they can hurt a young dog's back."

Chloe nodded. "I think she'd love to go to a real class, once she's old enough."

"Agility is great for collies; they're so bright and so energetic. And it uses up all that energy, too. They can be a real handful when they're bored."

Chloe nodded. "Jess was being so naughty before we came to training," she agreed. "She was a nightmare."

"You should definitely bring her to agility. Did you know some agility teachers run ABC classes?" Mike asked her, grinning. "Anything But Collies. Because they're so good at it, they leave all the other dogs in the dust!"

When they got back, Mom dashed out to meet them and hugged Chloe delightedly. "Will's coming home! Tomorrow! Isn't that wonderful?"

Chloe hugged her back. She had missed Will so much. Although it did hurt a little bit to see Jess jumping up and down, wagging her whole back end, not just her tail, she was so excited. "You're going to be so glad to see him, aren't you?" Chloe said, giving her a pet. "Will's hardly going to recognize you, your fur's so long now!"

After dinner, she spread herself out on the living-room floor and taped together six big sheets of drawing paper.

"There you are! What are you doing?" Dad asked, peering through the living-room door.

"Making a WELCOME HOME! banner for Will. I thought I'd put it in the hallway. Can I tie it to the banisters?"

"Of course you can. That's a really nice idea, Chlo. Do you need any help?"

Chloe shook her head. "Only with the tying. Thanks, Dad."

The banner took a long time: outlining the letters, then painting them in with lots of different colors. When she'd finished filling in WELCOME HOME! Chloe decided to take a break and go and get some juice while it dried.

She came back with her drink and stood at the door to admire her work— which was now decorated with a pattern of blue and red paw prints.

"Jess!" Chloe said. "You walked on it!"

Jess looked up at her guiltily, and gave her tail an apologetic wag. Chloe laughed. "Actually, I bet Will would like it better like this, anyway." She smiled to herself, imagining how furious she would have been if Jess had done something like that a few weeks ago. "You just want to welcome him back, too, don't you? We'd better wash your paws, though, before you track paint everywhere."

Jess and Chloe sat on the window seat, staring out at the road, waiting for Will to come. Jess kept jumping down, running over to the front door, and then dashing back again. She was so excited her tail couldn't stop wagging. Will! Chloe had said Will was coming home!

Chloe peered out of the window. "Yes! There's the car, Jess. They're here!"

Jess shot out into the hallway, barking excitedly and scrabbling at the door.

Chloe opened it, and they stood watching as Will struggled out of the car on his crutches.

Jess looked up at
Chloe uncertainly
as she saw Will
hobbling toward
them,
but Chloe
smiled and
shooed her
forward.
Will was
beaming and
calling to her, so she went to sniff him,
and then licked his hands lovingly. She
could tell that she shouldn't jump up.

"Good girl, Jess," Mom said gratefully.
"I was worried she might be a little
rough."

Will loved the banner. "Great
painting, Jess." He chuckled, balancing

on one crutch to ruffle her fur. He looked up at Chloe. "Thanks for looking after her. She looks great."

Chloe smiled proudly, but he was saying it as if she didn't have to worry anymore. It felt like Will was taking Jess back now. She lagged behind as they went into the house. Feeling as though she ought to let Will and Jess be on their own, she lingered in the hallway. She missed Jess already!

Jess led Will into the living room, and lay down determinedly on his lap as soon as he sat down on the sofa.

"She's not letting you go again," Dad said, laughing.

Jess sighed happily. But then she looked around for Chloe. Why wasn't she here, too?

Jess sat up and licked Will's hand, then headed out into the hallway, where Chloe was sitting on the stairs. Jess looked up at her and gave a worried little whine. Why was Chloe all on her own? She took the hem of Chloe's dress in her teeth and tugged very gently.

Chloe smiled at her, her eyes widening with hope. "You want me to come, too?" she whispered, and Jess wagged her tail. Chloe leaned forward and kissed the top of her head. "You belong to both of us now, don't you?" she whispered gratefully.

Chapter Eight

"Jess! Jess!" Chloe ran down the stairs, a worried edge creeping into her voice. She couldn't find Jess anywhere. Or Will. But she had a horrible feeling that she knew where they were.

Will had hated being stuck in the house over the last few days. Almost more than he'd hated the hospital. He couldn't ride his bike or skateboard, and even if he wanted to go upstairs Mom or Dad had to help. But not being able to walk Jess was the worst thing of all. He was desperate to take her out. Mom had driven him and Chloe to the park the day after he came back, so that he could watch Jess running around. But poor Jess hadn't understood, and she'd kept coming back to Will and staring at him hopefully, wanting him to join in.

Ever since then, Will had been aching to take Jess out to the park by himself.

"She's really well behaved now, Mom," he'd pleaded that morning at breakfast. "It isn't far. Now that she's been to dog-training classes, I could take her, no problem."

"Of course you can't!" Mom sounded horrified. "You're only just out of the hospital! You need to use your crutches; how can you possibly manage Jess as well?"

But Chloe didn't think Will had been convinced. He'd just scowled into his cereal.

Now, Chloe stopped dead at the bottom of the stairs, her eyes wide. Will's crutches were propped up by the front door, and Jess's leash was gone from its hook.

He'd taken her out, Chloe realized, nibbling her thumbnail anxiously. He'd gotten so angry with everyone fussing over him that he'd decided to show them, and he'd taken Jess for a walk on his own.

Chloe stared at the door. If she went and told, Mom would have a fit. Better to just go and find them. She reached for the house keys and quietly let herself outside.

Jess was walking beautifully, not pulling at all, just like she'd learned at the training classes. But Will was holding her leash strangely, she thought, looking up at him. He kept wobbling. He looked like he wanted to turn back, and they were only halfway to the park. Jess stared up at him and whimpered. Something was wrong.

Will suddenly sat down on someone's front wall, gasping. "Sorry, Jess," he muttered. "I shouldn't have brought you out; it was a stupid idea and now we're stuck."

Jess pulled gently at the leash in his hand, but he tightened his grip. "No, sorry, Jess. We're not going to the park."

Jess whined—she had to make him understand. If he let her go, she could fetch help! She took the leash in her teeth this time and tugged at it harder. Then she walked a couple of steps back in the direction of the house and barked encouragingly at him.

"No, I can't," Will tried to explain. "Oh! *You* want to go home? Do you know the way?" he asked doubtfully.

Home! Jess sat down, wagging her tail. She pulled the leash with her teeth again, and this time he let it go.

"Go home, Jess. Find Chloe," Will told her. The puppy licked his hand reassuringly before trotting off down the road as fast as she could. She felt anxious—she didn't like running along with her leash trailing like this. But she had to help Will.

Chloe dashed down their street, heading for the park. She really hoped Will hadn't done anything to make his leg worse. What if he'd fallen?

Suddenly, she spotted Jess running toward her—on her own. Where was Will?

Jess gave a delighted bark. She'd found Chloe! She jumped up at her, barking again and again, and Chloe hugged her tightly. "Good girl, Jess. Shhh! Where's Will? Can you show me?" she asked, holding Jess's scrabbly front paws.

Jess jumped down immediately and turned back, waiting for Chloe to pick up her leash. Then they raced along the road together.

Will was still sitting on the wall when Jess proudly led Chloe back to him. He was looking very white, and Chloe sat down next to him, wondering if he'd be angry at her if she gave him a hug. She compromised by putting an arm around his shoulder.

"Don't say it," he muttered.

"I didn't!"

Will smiled at her for a second. "Sorry. I should have listened to Mom. It's a good thing Jess was here. She knew what to do—she made me let go of the leash so she could fetch you."

"She's a star," Chloe told him, watching Jess panting contently. "You should come to her training classes, you know. The last beginners' class is on Thursday. It's a special competition. You'd be really proud of her." She stood up and helped him pull himself to his feet. Then they set off slowly down the road.

"Um, maybe," Will said quietly. "I'm sorry I was so jealous before. It's just that I was looking forward to taking her."

"You could help me practice with her," Chloe suggested. "Even if the walking parts are difficult, you could do sit and stay. And she needs to learn to behave properly for you, too."

"I suppose so." Will looked more cheerful. "Granddad told me about her stealing that lady's groceries. They ought to have a food hunt in this competition. Jess would win, wouldn't you?"

Jess barked, ears pricked, and Will burst out laughing.

"I'm never taking her anywhere near a store ever again." Chloe shuddered. "Come on. If we're quick, Mom might not have noticed we've been gone."

They limped back home, with Jess walking at a snail's pace beside them, giving them both loving looks.

"I can't believe how good she is!" Will told Chloe, as he watched Jess sitting on her own in the middle of the room, with a biscuit between her front paws. "She isn't even looking at it!"

"She knows she'll get it in a minute," Chloe said, but she couldn't keep the proud smile off her face. "All that practice we've done has really helped."

Mike nodded at her, and she walked back to Jess. "Good girl!" she said. "You can eat it now."

Jess gulped down the treat happily. She could see Will grinning at her, too.

Mike wrote something on the piece of paper he was holding and looked around the room. "Well done, everyone! That's the end of the competition, so if you can all line up along here with your dogs, please, I'll announce the winners."

Chloe grabbed Will's arm and helped him to the center of the hall, so that he could line up with Jess, too.

"She's your dog as well," she hissed, as he gave her an *I shouldn't be doing this!* look. "Intermediate training classes start next week, and I told Mike we're both coming—we can take turns leashing her. You can be off your crutches for an hour by then, can't you?"

Will nodded, grinning. "I'm sure I'll manage it."

Mike was walking along the line with a handful of shiny ribbons. "Well, it's been very tight, but we have a winner. Chloe and Will, can you bring Jess out for her first-place ribbon, please!"

"Jess, you won!" Chloe hugged her, quickly rubbing her cheek against Jess's silky ruff of fur. "Come on, Will!"

As they made their way to the front, Chloe looked over delightedly at Mom and Dad and Granddad, all clapping. Granddad had the camera ready, too.

Mike handed Chloe the ribbon, and she bent down to pin it to Jess's collar. The puppy looked up at Will on one side and Chloe on the other, both smiling. And she thumped her tail happily on the floor.

KITTY CORNER

Where kitties get the love they need

These
purr-fect
kittens
need a
home!

KITTY CORNER

Where kitties get the love they need

CALLIE

ELLEN MILES

SCHOLASTIC

KITTY CORNER

Where Kitties get the love they need

OTIS

ELLEN MILES

SCHOLASTIC

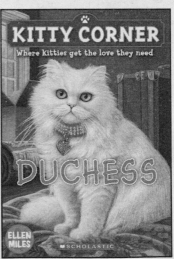

KITTY CORNER

Where Kitties get the love they need

DUCHESS

ELLEN MILES

SCHOLASTIC